FROM SEED TO PUMPKIN

BY WENDY PFEFFER

ILLUSTRATED BY JAMES GRAHAM HALE

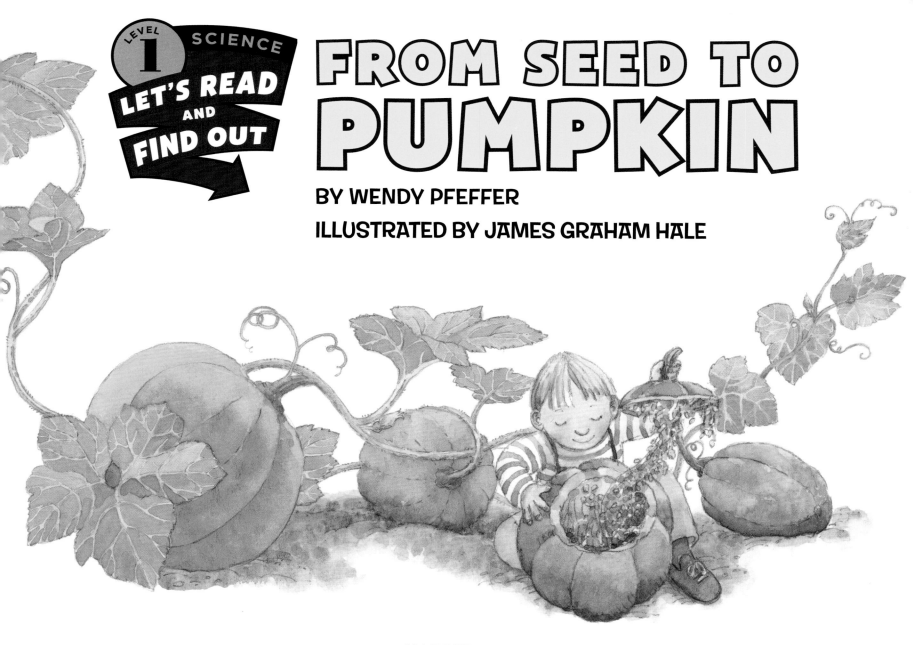

HARPER

An Imprint of HarperCollinsPublishers

With thanks to Barbara J. Bromley,
Mercer County Horticulturist,
for sharing her vast knowledge of plants,
and with sincere appreciation to
Sarah Thomson for her valuable guidance

The Let's-Read-and-Find-Out Science book series was originated by Dr. Franklyn M. Branley, Astronomer Emeritus and former Chairman of the American Museum of Natural History–Hayden Planetarium, and was formerly co-edited by him and Dr. Roma Gans, Professor Emeritus of Childhood Education, Teachers College, Columbia University. Text and illustrations for each of the books in the series are checked for accuracy by an expert in the relevant field. For more information about Let's-Read-and-Find-Out Science books, write to HarperCollins Children's Books, 195 Broadway, New York, NY 10007, or visit our website at www.letsreadandfindout.com.

Let's Read-and-Find-Out Science® is a trademark of HarperCollins Publishers.
From Seed to Pumpkin
Text copyright © 2004 by Wendy Pfeffer
Illustrations copyright © 2004 by James Graham Hale
All rights reserved. Manufactured in China.
No part of this book may be used or reproduced in any manner whatsoever without written permission except in the case of brief quotation embodied in critical articles and reviews. For information address HarperCollins Children's Books, a division of HarperCollins Publishers, 195 Broadway, New York, NY 10007.
www.harpercollinschildrens.com

Library of Congress Cataloging-in-Publication Data
Pfeffer, Wendy.
    From seed to pumpkin / by Wendy Pfeffer ; illustrated by James Graham Hale.
       p.   cm. — (Let's-read-and-find-out science. Stage 1)
    ISBN 978-0-06-238185-9
    1. Pumpkin—Life cycles—Juvenile literature.   [1. Pumpkin.]   I. Hale, James Graham, ill.   II. Title.
III. Series.
SB347.P44   2004   583'.63—dc21   00-054039

15 16 17 18 19   SCP   10 9 8 7 6 5 4 3 2 1   ❖   Revised edition, 2015

For Phil, Diane, Tim, and Jaime,
who grow all kinds of good food,
as well as great pumpkins
—W.P.

When spring winds warm the earth, a farmer plants hundreds of pumpkin seeds.

Every pumpkin seed can become a baby pumpkin plant. Underground, covered with dark, moist soil, the baby plants begin to grow.

As the plants get bigger, the seeds crack open. Stems sprout up. Roots dig down. Inside the roots are tubes. Water travels up these tubes the way juice goes up a straw.

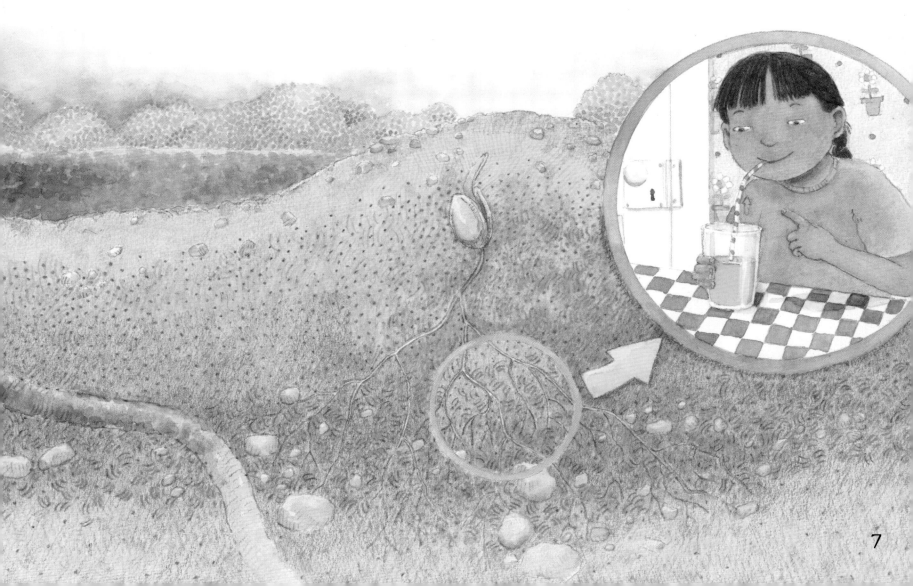

In less than two weeks from planting time, green shoots poke up through the earth.

The pumpkins are ripe and round, with lumps and bumps.
They come in all sizes and shapes. And they're waiting in the
autumn sun.

Some pumpkins will be carved into jack-o'-lanterns for Halloween.

Some will be baked into pumpkin pies for Thanksgiving.

Colorful leaves turn brown. Winter winds begin to blow, and soon the trees are bare. The farmer looks out over the pumpkin patch, where only a few dead vines remain.

30

But when spring winds warm the earth, once again he will plant hundreds of pumpkin seeds. And once again, they will grow—from seed to pumpkin.

31

FIND OUT MORE ABOUT PUMPKINS

- Did You Know a Pumpkin Is a Fruit?

The seed-bearing part of any flowering plant is called its fruit. Because a pumpkin has seeds in the middle it is really a fruit. Tomatoes, cucumbers, and pea pods are fruits, too. Because they are not sweet like other fruits we often call them vegetables.

- Roasted Pumpkin Seeds

When you carve your jack-o'-lantern, save the seeds you scoop out. Wash the pulp off. Then let them dry. Pumpkin seeds are filled with vitamins and minerals, so they are good to eat.

You will need:

1 cup of pumpkin seeds   2 teaspoons cooking oil
paper towels   mixing bowl
1/2 teaspoon salt   cookie sheet

1. Ask an adult to help.
2. Preheat oven to 350° F.
3. Wash seeds and pat dry between paper towels.
4. Mix seeds, salt, and cooking oil together in a bowl.
5. Spread mixture on cookie sheet.
6. Bake 15 minutes. Stir. Bake 15 minutes more.
7. Let them cool. Then enjoy the crispy golden treats.

• How Plants Drink Water

Pumpkin roots have tubes. They drink water from the ground the way you drink water with a straw. A celery stalk has tubes, too. They are also connected to roots, so the celery plant can drink water from the ground. You can see how the tubes in a stalk of celery work.

You will need:

several celery stalks
a sharp knife
red or blue food coloring
a glass, half full of water

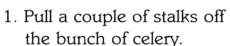

1. Pull a couple of stalks off the bunch of celery.
2. Ask an adult to help you cut them straight across the bottom.
3. Pour a few drops of red or blue coloring in the water and stir.
4. Place the celery stalks in the water with the cut ends down.
5. Wait about an hour.
6. See how the colored water has gone up the tubes in the celery.
7. Take one of the stalks of celery from the water and break it in half.
8. Look for the tubes now. See how the colored water has traveled up them.